KUNG POW CHICKEN★
THE BIRDY SNATCHERS

Cyndi Marko

BRANCHES™
SCHOLASTIC INC.

For Bowie,
who's a total smarty-pants

No part of this publication may be reproduced, stored in a retrieval system, or transmitted in any form or by any means, electronic, mechanical, photocopying, recording, or otherwise, without written permission of the publisher. For information regarding permission, write to Scholastic Inc., Attention: Permissions Department, 557 Broadway, New York, NY 10012.

Library of Congress Cataloging-in-Publication Data

Marko, Cyndi, author.
The birdy snatchers / by Cyndi Marko.
pages cm. — (Kung Pow Chicken ; 3)
Summary: Superheroes Kung Pow Chicken and Egg Drop must stop the evil Birdbrain from zapping the smartest chickens in Fowladelphia into zombies.
ISBN 0-545-61068-0 (pbk. : alk. paper) — ISBN 0-545-61072-9 (hardcover : alk. paper) — ISBN 0-545-61393-0 (ebook) 1. Superheroes — Juvenile fiction. 2. Chickens — Juvenile fiction. 3. Supervillains — Juvenile fiction. 4. Zombies — Juvenile fiction. [1. Superheroes — Fiction. 2. Chickens — Fiction. 3. Supervillains — Fiction. 4. Zombies — Fiction. 5. Humorous stories.] I. Title.
PZ7.M33968Bi 2014
[Fic] — dc23
2013046294
ISBN 978-0-545-61072-8 (hardcover) / ISBN 978-0-545-61068-1 (paperback)

10 9 8 7 6 5 4 3 2 1   14 15 16 17 18 19/0

Printed in China

First Scholastic printing, August 2014

38

TABLE OF CONTENTS

Gordon's room

lunch box

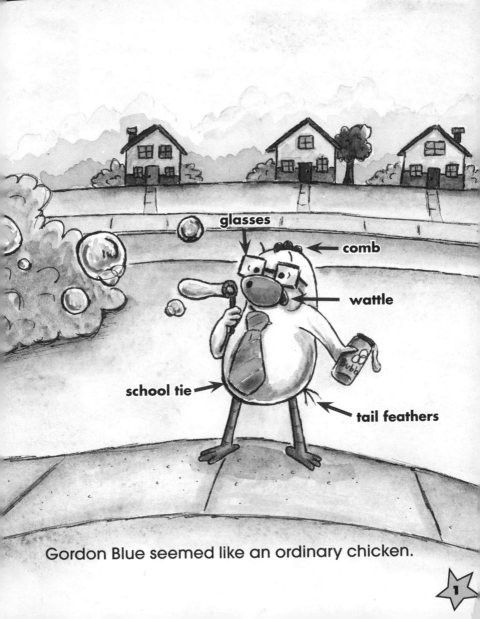

glasses

comb

wattle

school tie

tail feathers

Gordon Blue seemed like an ordinary chicken.

He lived with his ordinary family in the city of Fowladelphia.

It was an ordinary city. (Except for all the bad guys.)

And Gordon went to an ordinary school with other ordinary chickens.

But Gordon had a <u>super</u> secret.

When Gordon was younger, he fell into a vat of toxic sludge! Uncle Quack rescued him.

But the toxic sludge had given Gordon superpowers.

If bad guys are up to no good, Gordon's tail feathers tingle.

-Tingle!

Mwa-Ha!-Ha!

Then he slips into his super suit to fight bad guys as:

Super-suit

super hard shell

KUNG POW CHICKEN!

With his sidekick, Egg Drop!

Being a superhero wasn't easy.

Gordon liked having superpowers. But he wanted to meet other superheroes he could ask about super stuff.

Gordon liked catching bad guys. But it was tricky chasing them when his mom was around.

Kung Pow Chicken had already battled two bad guys. He had saved the city twice! Now Fowladelphia was quiet and safe.

With no bad guys to fight, Kung Pow Chicken was old news.

There you are, Gordon—under that ad for beak wax.

Beaky's
Beak
Wax

SALE

LET YOUR
BEAK SHINE THROUGH

$REWARD$

I, Sam Snood, still want to know who Kung Pow Chicken really is. Call me.

Snoopy reporter Sam Snood had found another chicken for the front page.

THE FOWL TIMES

GAME SHOW GOOF-UP

Sam Snood
Junior
Reporter

A wannabe smarty-chicken named Birdbrain scored the lowest score EVER on the quiz show <u>Quiz Whiz</u>. Birdbrain said, "I'm a very brainy bird. I work at the zoo. That's a smarty-pants place. It is this show's questions that are dumb. I'm pretty sure cats moo!"

SMARTY-PANTS CLUB MEETING

When?
2 P.M. Thursday!

Where?
The Coffee Coop!

Who?
Club members!

There were no bad guys to catch. So Gordon was <u>super</u> bored. He was starting to wonder if he would be bored for the rest of his life.

Gordon got ready for another ordinary day at
school.

Mrs. Blue squeezed Gordon and Benny tight.

The walk to school was a bit strange.

Is it Pajama Day?

Gordon dropped Benny off at kindergarten.

Then he walked to his second grade
classroom. He sat next to his friend Annie.

Gordon's teacher, Mr. Giblets, was writing on the board.

The classroom speaker crackled. Gordon and his classmates grew quiet. They waited for their principal to give the morning news.

Good morning, Sunnyside School! All students are to leave right now. GO HOME! Teachers, come to the food-eating room. NOW! That is all. Have a nice day.

Gordon, that wasn't the principal's voice!

TINGLE!

Gordon's birdy senses started to tingle. A bad guy was up to no good.

Mr. Giblets left the classroom. He didn't say good-bye to his students. He just kept bokking about brains.

Gordon peeked out the door. Mr. Giblets and the rest of the teachers were shuffling down the hallway to the lunchroom. They were ALL acting weird.

BRAINS!

Mrs. Featherbee

First Grade

103

Gordon <u>had</u> to find his little brother! It was superhero time.

Gordon ran to Benny's classroom.

The brothers found a good place to hide.

Gordon opened his lunch box.

LET'S GET CRACKING!

Finally!

Kung Pow Chicken and Egg Drop tiptoed down the hallway. They heard something weird.

Then they tiptoed inside.

They belly-crawled over to the lunch counter and hid behind a jumbo-size can of creamed corn. But they weren't alone.

Kung Pow Chicken didn't know Birdbrain's plan. But he knew Birdbrain <u>had</u> to be stopped. He told Annie to stay put. Then he flashed his Drumsticks of Doom. It was time to get cracking.

Kung Pow Chicken and Egg Drop jumped out from behind the creamed corn.

Kung Pow Chicken, Egg Drop, and Annie burst out of the kitchen. They ran down the hallway. The zombies were right on their tail feathers!

The superheroes and Annie ran outside. Kung Pow Chicken held the doors shut. Egg Drop pushed a hockey stick through the handles. The zombies would have to find another way out.

Well, that was weird!

Yeah! What kind of bad guy doesn't want to battle?

The kind who has an army of zombies?

Kung Pow Chicken took out his Beak-Phone. He hit the AUTO-BEAK button. The Beak-Mobile showed up right away.

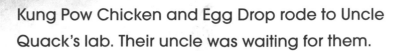

Kung Pow Chicken and Egg Drop rode to Uncle
Quack's lab. Their uncle was waiting for them.

Uncle Quack held up a copy of the Fowl Times.

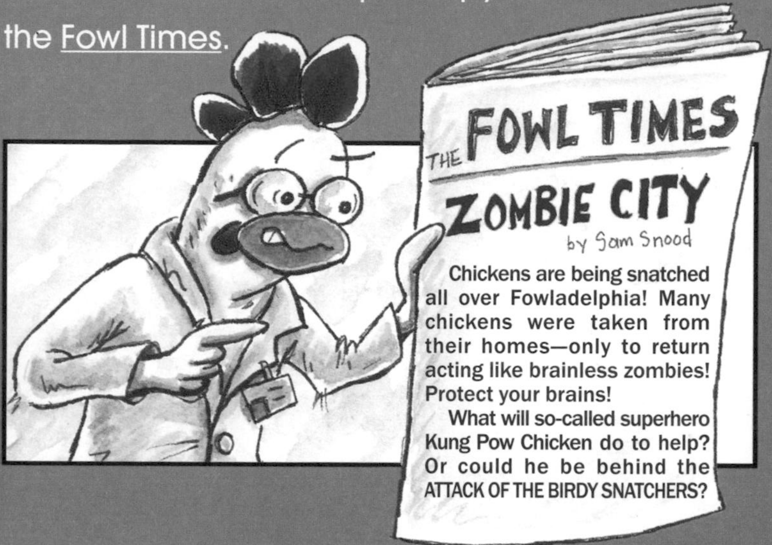

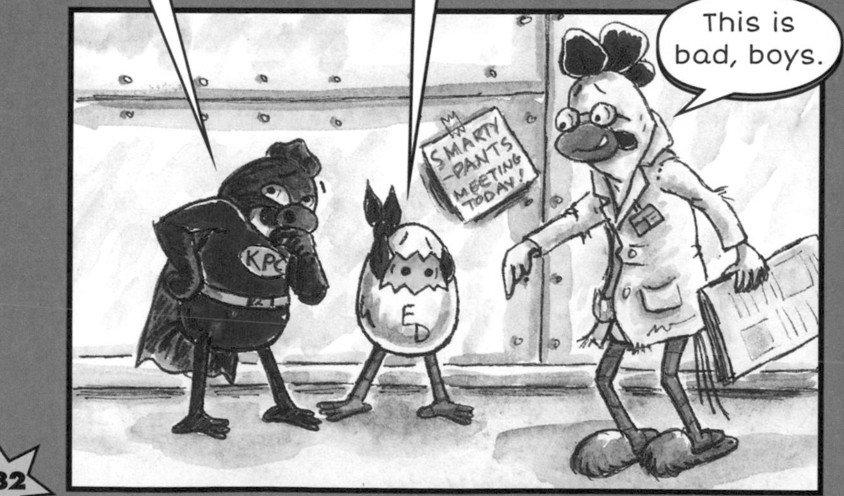

They didn't know what Birdbrain was up to. But they did all agree that zombies were bad. The heroes needed to find out more about Birdbrain and about zombies.

Uncle Quack grabbed two shiny helmets.

He put them on his nephews' heads.

Zombies can smell brain waves. These Zom-B-Gones™ muffle your brain waves. So brain-hungry zombies won't be able to sniff you out.

Thanks, Uncle Quack!

Are these made of <u>tinfoil</u>?

Kung Pow Chicken and Egg Drop's brains were safe from zombies. They were ready to catch the bad guy! They just had to find his hideout.

The heroes said good-bye to Uncle Quack.

Bring back a zombie for my See-Thru-U™ machine! I'd love to see inside his head!

Okay. And see what you can find out about Birdbrain while we go after him.

To the Beak-Mobile!

Birdy Snatched!

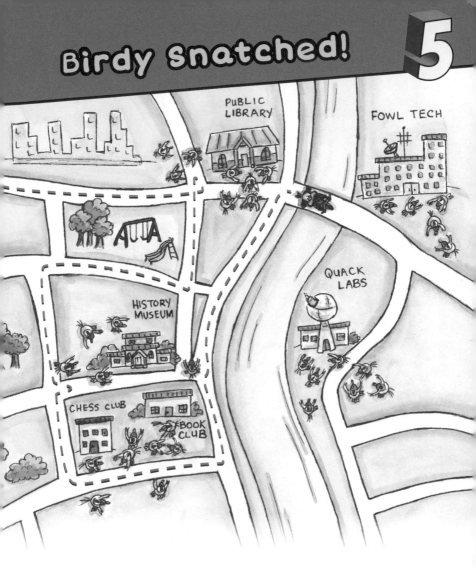

The superheroes rode up and down the city
streets. Brain-hungry zombies were everywhere!
They were at the Public Library, the Chess Club,
and even the smarty-college, Fowl Tech.

RIIING!

Kung Pow Chicken answered his Beak-Phone. It was Annie Beakly.

Hey. I did a Gaggle search and found clues. Not only did Birdbrain get EVERY question wrong on that game show, but he was booed off the stage! AND he <u>tried</u> to join the Smarty-Pants Club. But after that show, they wouldn't let him in.

Thanks, Annie!

Kung Pow Chicken told Annie to stay safe. He put away his Beak-Phone.

The heroes kept driving. Soon they spotted a noisy pack of zombies by Uncle Quack's lab. The brain-hungry zombies had snatched Uncle Quack!

Kung Pow Chicken zoomed the Beak-Mobile through the zombie mob. Zombies scrambled out of the way.

Egg Drop snatched his uncle away from the zombies. But it was too late: Uncle Quack was a zombie.

Kung Pow Chicken and Egg Drop zoomed to the lab. They sat their uncle down behind the See-Thru-U™ machine. Egg Drop turned it on.

Phew! His brain is still there!

His BRAIN! Wait a minute! That's it! Uncle Quack is the biggest brain in town! Birdbrain's zombies aren't snatching BRAINS, they're snatching BRAINY chickens!

KPC

DANGER

Kung Pow Chicken called Annie. She showed up right away. Then the heroes went looking for zombies.

Kung Pow Chicken and Egg Drop spotted a pack of zombies. They parked the Beak-Mobile and followed the zombies around the corner.

The heroes came beak-to-beak with a huge zombie army!

Kung Pow Chicken tried to escape. But the zombies lifted him up into the air. They grabbed Egg Drop, too.

The heroes had been birdy snatched!

But the zombies couldn't sniff the heroes' brains through their helmets. So Egg Drop snatched the Zom-B-Gone™ from Kung Pow Chicken's head. He took his own off, too.

Ack! What are you doing?!

Trust me!

The zombies smelled brains.

BOK!

BOK!

BRAINS!

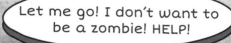

Let me go! I don't want to be a zombie! HELP!

BRAINS!

BOK!

KPC

For peep's sake, Kung Pow! The zombies will take us to Birdbrain. We'll put the Zom-B-Gones™ back on before he can turn us into zombies.

Kung Pow Chicken stopped struggling.

After a long march, the zombies stopped at the Fowladelphia Zoo. They dumped Kung Pow Chicken and Egg Drop in an empty pit. The heroes were trapped!

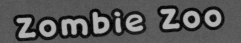

Zombie Zoo

Kung Pow Chicken and Egg Drop put their Zom-B-Gones™ back on. They huddled on an iceberg.

Of course the zoo is Birdbrain's hideout. He works here!

We got snatched for nothing.

But zombie surfing was worth it!

BRRR!

BRRR!

Birdbrain held up a strange-looking gadget.

Now I'm going to the Smarty-Pants Club meeting! But first, I'll use my Zombie-Zapper to zap you two into zombies.

Birdbrain zapped Kung Pow Chicken
and Egg Drop. The heroes
were blown backward
by the blast!

But Uncle Quack's Zom-B-Gones™ had kept their brains safe.

Birdbrain fell for their zombie act. Then he and his zombies left the zoo.

Kung Pow Chicken and Egg Drop were stuck on the iceberg. But at least they weren't zombies. They took off their helmets.

Suddenly, the Chicken-Wing™ swooped down from the sky. It passed over Kung Pow Chicken and Egg Drop.

The mystery flyer snagged the heroes and lifted them up into the air!

The Chicken-Wing™ landed outside the zoo.

Kung Pow Chicken and Egg Drop turned to face their rescuer. A superhero stood before them. Or, it was a chicken <u>dressed</u> like a superhero.

Kung Pow Chicken was happy to be rescued. But he was <u>not</u> happy to see Annie. Now he was cranky.

What are <u>you</u> doing here?

I was zombie-sitting Professor Quack. Then you "pocket dialed" me from your Beak-Phone. When I heard Birdbrain zap you, I just had to help!

But you should be keeping Professor Quack safe!

Oh, he's fine. I put him in his empty pool with a beach ball.

Kung Pow is ALWAYS sitting on his phone!

There was a bad guy on the loose. Kung Pow Chicken didn't have time to bok at Beak Girl.

We need to find Birdbrain and get his Zombie-Zapper. Then we can zap the zombies back to normal.

Birdbrain said he was going to the Smarty-Pants Club meeting!

And the Fowl Times said the meeting is at the Coffee Coop!

To the Coffee Coop!

The three heroes burst into the Coffee Coop. But they were too late. Birdbrain had already zapped all the Smarty-Pants Club members with his Zombie-Zapper! The heroes were outnumbered.

Annie hid under a table. Kung Pow Chicken flung the Beak-A-Rang. It knocked the zapper out of Birdbrain's hands.

The zombies swarmed Kung Pow Chicken and Egg Drop. The heroes didn't have their Zom-B-Gones™ to keep them safe. They tried to fight back. There were just too many zombies.

But Beak Girl couldn't bear to see her heroes in trouble. She grabbed the Zombie-Zapper.

Kung Pow Chicken quickly turned the dial to
CHICKEN. He pressed the button and spun in
a circle.

NOOOOOO!

ZAP!

ZAP!

ZAP!

ZAP!

ZAP!

Kung Pow Chicken turned the dial again—
this time to ZOMBIE. He zapped Birdbrain with the
Zombie-Zapper.

Kung Pow Chicken, Egg Drop, and Beak Girl rushed to the lab to zap Uncle Quack. They told him everything.

Beak Girl took off her mask. She was just ordinary Annie Beakly again.

Thanks for your help, Annie. But you don't have superpowers to keep you safe. Next time, leave the bad-guy fighting to the <u>real</u> superheroes.

Hmmph. Well, I <u>did</u> save your tail feathers twice today!

Maybe she needs a sidekick?

After Annie left, the heroes put away their super suits. Another bad egg had been cracked—just in time for dinner.

I can't wait for dessert!

KUNG POW CHICKEN ★

Prove your superhero know-how!

Look at the picture on page 13. Why is Gordon's walk to school stranger than normal?

Why is Birdbrain turning chickens into zombies?

How does Beak Girl help Kung Pow Chicken and Egg Drop? How do Kung Pow Chicken and Egg Drop feel about her?

What is the difference between the words <u>smart</u> and <u>smartest</u>? What does the suffix <u>-est</u> mean?

Pretend you are a sidekick like Egg Drop. Design your costume and describe your superpower.

Zom-B-Gone™

blanket fort

Cyndi Marko lives in Canada with her family.

When Cyndi was little, she loved scary stories. She got the heebie-jeebies reading monster books under her blankets. And the best scary stories were always the ones about brain-hungry zombies. Those really creeped her out! Now that Cyndi is bigger, she's a chicken when it comes to scary stories. But she still loves reading about zombies—as long as she's wearing her brain-smell-blocking Zom-B-Gone™.

Kung Pow Chicken is Cyndi's first children's book series.

← scary books

scary story snacks